D0049004

Teachers, librarians, and kids from across Canada are talking about the *Canadian Flyer Adventures.* Here's what some of them had to say:

Great Canadian historical content, excellent illustrations, and superb closing historical facts (I love the kids' commentary!). ~ SARA S., TEACHER, ONTARIO

As a teacher–librarian I welcome this series with open arms. It fills the gap for Canadian historical adventures at an early reading level! There's fast action, interesting, believable characters, and great historical information. ~ MARGARET L., TEACHER–LIBRARIAN, BRITISH COLUMBIA

The *Canadian Flyer Adventures* will transport young readers to different eras of our past with their appealing topics. Thank goodness there are more artifacts in that old dresser ... they are sure to lead to even more escapades. ~ SALLY B., TEACHER–LIBRARIAN, MANITOBA

When I shared the book with a grade 1–2 teacher at my school, she enjoyed the book, noting that her students would find it appealing because of the action-adventure and short chapters. ~ HEATHER J., TEACHER AND LIBRARIAN, NOVA SCOTIA

Newly independent readers will fly through each *Canadian Flyer Adventure*, and be asking for the next installment! Children will enjoy the fast-paced narrative, the personalities of the main characters, and the drama of the dangerous situations the children find themselves in. ~ PAM L., LIBRARIAN, ONTARIO

I love the fact that these are Canadian adventures—kids should know how exciting Canadian history is. Emily and Matt are regular kids, full of curiosity, and I can see readers relating to them. ~ *JEAN K., TEACHER, ONTARIO*

What kids told us:

I would like to have the chance to ride on a magical sled and have adventures. ~ *EMMANUEL*

I would like to tell the author that her book is amazing, incredible, awesome, and a million times better than any book I've read. ~ *MARIA*

I would recommend the *Canadian Flyer Adventures* series to other kids so they could learn about Canada too. The book is just the right length and hard to put down. ~ *PAUL*

The books I usually read are the full-of-fact encyclopedias. This book is full of interesting ideas that simply grab me. ~ *ELEANOR*

At the end of the book Matt and Emily say they are going on another adventure. I'm very interested in where they are going next! ~ *ALEX*

I like when Emily and Matt fly into the sky on a sled towards a new adventure. I can't wait for the next book! ~ *JI SANG*

Make It Fair!

Frieda Wishinsky

Illustrated by Patricia Ann Lewis-MacDougall

MAPLE
TREE
PRESS

For my friend Kady MacDonald Denton

Many thanks to the hard-working Owlkids team, for their insightful comments
and steadfast support. Special thanks to Patricia Ann Lewis-MacDougall
and Barb Kelly for their engaging and energetic illustrations and design.

Maple Tree books are published by Owlkids Books Inc.
10 Lower Spadina Avenue, Suite 400, Toronto, Ontario M5V 2Z2
www.owlkids.com

Text © 2010 Frieda Wishinsky
Illustrations © 2010 Patricia Ann Lewis-MacDougall

Distributed in Canada by Raincoast Books
9050 Shaughnessy Street, Vancouver, British Columbia V6P 6E5

Distributed in the United States by Publishers Group West
1700 Fourth Street, Berkeley, California 94710

Library and Archives Canada Cataloguing in Publication

Wishinsky, Frieda
Make it fair! / Frieda Wishinsky ; illustrated by
Patricia Ann Lewis-MacDougall.

(Canadian flyer adventures ; 15)
Issued also in an electronic format.
ISBN 978-1-897349-98-4 (bound).--ISBN 978-1-897349-99-1 (pbk.)

1. McClung, Nellie L., 1873-1951--Juvenile fiction. I. Lewis-
MacDougall, Patricia Ann II. Title. III. Series: Wishinsky, Frieda.
Canadian flyer adventures ; 15.

PS8595.I834M36 2010   jC813'.54   C2010-904703-6

Library of Congress Control Number: 2010931640

 Canada Council   Conseil des Arts
for the Arts   du Canada   ONTARIO ARTS COUNCIL
CONSEIL DES ARTS DE L'ONTARIO

We acknowledge the financial support of the Canada Council for the Arts,
the Ontario Arts Council, the Government of Canada through the
Canada Book Fund (CBF), and the Government of Ontario through
the Ontario Media Development Corporation's Book Initiative
for our publishing activities.

Manufactured by Friesens Corporation
Manufactured in Altona, MB, Canada in September 2010
Job# 59219

A   B   C   D   E   F

CONTENTS

HOW IT ALL BEGAN

Emily and Matt couldn't believe their luck. They discovered an old dresser full of strange objects in the tower of Emily's house. They also found a note from Emily's Great-Aunt Miranda: "The sled is yours. Fly it to wonderful adventures."

They found a sled right behind the dresser! When they sat on it, shimmery gold words appeared:

Rub the leaf
Three times fast.
Soon you'll fly
To the past.

The sled rose over Emily's house. It flew over their town of Glenwood. It sailed out of a cloud and into the past. Their adventures on the flying sled had begun! Where will the sled take them next? Turn the page to find out.

1

Right This Way

Emily paraded up and down her porch waving a white sign. "Fight for rights! Give women the vote!"

"Why are you marching for women's rights, Em?" called her best friend Matt. He bounded up the porch stairs. "Women have rights. They can vote."

"They can *now*. But they couldn't vote in the early 1900s. In those days men controlled everything. It was *so* unfair."

"But why are you protesting now?"

"Because I'm playing Nellie McClung in a class skit for Women's History Month. She fought for women's rights."

"That's great. How did she fight?" asked Matt.

"She put on a play in 1914."

Matt laughed. "Yeah, right. A play doesn't change anything."

Emily wrinkled her nose. "It does if you're funny and smart and make people understand that laws can be dumb and unfair."

"That must have been some awesome play."

"It was. I wish I could have seen it. Then I'd know how to act in my skit."

"Maybe you can see it. The magic sled might fly us to meet Nellie McClung."

2

Emily's eyes sparkled. "You're right! Let's check it out!"

Emily dropped her sign on a chair. The friends scooted up the back stairs to Emily's tower room.

She ran to the dresser and opened the first drawer. They peered inside.

"Nothing here," said Matt.

"Wait!" said Emily. "There is something."

Emily pulled out a yellowing pamphlet from the left corner of the drawer. "Wow! It says, *Fight for rights with Nellie. It's only right!*"

"Great!" said Matt. "Let's go!"

Emily lifted the sled from behind the dresser. "Do you have your digital recorder with you?"

"Here in my pocket. And do you have your sketchbook?"

"Right here!" Emily tapped the pocket of her jeans.

The friends hopped on the sled. Immediately, shimmery gold words appeared.

Rub the leaf
Three times fast.
Soon you'll fly
To the past.

Instantly fog enveloped the sled. When the clouds lifted, Emily and Matt were flying.

"This sled is the best," said Emily as they sailed over Glenwood and into a fluffy white cloud. "I love flying, even if my stomach somersaults each time we go up."

"And my stomach somersaults each time we go down," said Matt, gulping. "Like right now!"

2
That Man

The sled bumped down in front of a large building. Snow glistened on the ground and on top of the building.

"What do you think this building is? It looks important," said Emily.

"There's a plaque. It says 'Manitoba Legislature'."

"Brrrr," said Emily, sliding off the sled. "Why didn't the sled fly us inside? I'm glad we're dressed for the weather, at least."

Emily wore a long navy blue wool coat,

a green hat, mittens, and high black boots. Matt wore long pants, a thick jacket, mittens, a cap, and black boots.

The friends scurried up the steps and into the building. Their footsteps echoed down the long hall.

They could hear voices in one of the rooms. They ran over and opened the door. The large chamber was packed with people.

"Look! There are women sitting at a table in front. Maybe one of them is Nellie McClung," said Emily.

"Get out of here!" snapped a bearded man who was standing at the back. "Can't you see there are no seats? There's not even enough room to stand. Go upstairs to the gallery with the women and the press."

"He didn't have to be so rude," said Emily as they left.

"I know. Let's hurry upstairs. This way."
Matt pointed to a large staircase leading
upstairs. They opened a door and tiptoed into
a crowded gallery.

They sat down in the back as a woman in a
long dress and small hat rose from a chair at
the front of the hall.

"It's Nellie McClung! I'm sure of it," said
Emily. "But she's not putting on a play. She's
making a speech."

Nellie spoke in a clear, firm voice. She told

the audience that women are entitled to the vote. She poked fun at politicians and the unfair way they treated women.

The women in the gallery laughed and applauded.

When Nellie sat down, a man in a black suit stood up. He had a moustache, and he puffed out his chest like he was wearing a jacket full of medals.

"I bet that's Premier Roblin," Emily whispered to Matt, "I've seen his picture in my book."

"In England, women's rights have put people and property in danger," Roblin barked. He wagged his finger in the air as if he were scolding a roomful of naughty children.

"How dare Roblin speak about women in that insulting manner?" whispered a woman beside Emily.

"The nerve of that man!" said a woman beside Matt.

The women in the gallery muttered, grumbled, and glared at the premier. But the premier didn't hear or care. "Giving women the rights they seek will ruin family life," he blasted. "For every marriage in the United States there is a divorce."

"That's a lie," shouted a woman sitting below Emily and Matt. She stood up and waved a fist at the premier.

"It's rubbish!" proclaimed another woman. She rose to her feet, too.

"Tell Roblin what you think of him and his ideas, Nellie!" yelled a third woman. "Tell him! We're behind you!"

Emily and Matt peered down at Nellie. What was she going to say to Premier Roblin? Would she yell at him, too?

3

Just Kids

But Nellie didn't say a word to Premier Roblin. She just smiled sweetly at him.

"Why doesn't Mrs. McClung speak up?" said a man sitting in the row just below Matt and Emily. He had a moustache and he took notes as he spoke.

"That man must be a reporter," Matt whispered to Emily.

"I'm going to check Roblin's facts when I get back to the office, Earl," said a man wearing glasses beside the first man. "I'm sure he's wrong. There haven't been more divorces in the U.S. since women got rights."

"So why doesn't Nellie tell Roblin he's talking nonsense?" sneered Earl. "What do you think, Ken? Is she scared of him?"

"I bet she is," said Ken, adjusting his glasses. "Roblin's got power. Big power."

Emily leaned toward the two reporters.

"Mrs. McClung is not scared," she said.

"That's right," said a girl of about fourteen sitting beside the reporters. "I know that for sure."

"How do you know so much? Who are you?" asked Ken.

"I am Florence McClung, and my mother isn't afraid of anything or anyone. Wait till tomorrow. Then you'll see what women can do."

"You mean that play over at the Walker Theatre? What is that all about anyway?

What's your mother going to do in the show?"

"Come see the play and you'll find out," said Florence.

"Come on. Give me and Ken a hint," coaxed Earl. He winked at Florence.

"We won't tell anyone," said Ken.

"I'm not telling you anything else," said Florence.

Earl's eyes narrowed. "Listen, young lady," he snapped. "Things could get dangerous tomorrow. Not everyone agrees with your mother. Anything could happen."

Florence's face turned white. "Why would anyone want to hurt my mother? She's a good person."

"There are a lot of angry people who don't want women to vote," said Ken. "You never know what an angry person will do. Someone could get hurt."

"Stop scaring her," said Emily. "Anyway, aren't reporters supposed to sit with the press? Why are you sitting in the women's gallery?"

"We wanted to hear the women's point of view," said Earl. "So come on, talk to us, Florence. We're on your side."

"I...I..." stammered Florence.

"You don't have to tell them anything," said

Matt. "Not if you don't want to."

Earl glared at Emily and Matt. "Mind your own business. You don't know anything. You're just kids."

"But we're not stupid. And we know that Nellie McClung is brave and smart," said Emily.

"And we're all standing up with her," said Matt.

Florence smiled at Emily and Matt. "Yes! We will succeed! We'll all fight for what is right."

"And you'll lose," said Ken. "You can't fight powerful politicians like Premier Roblin."

4

Every Word

"Thank you," said Florence to Emily and Matt when the speeches were over.

"We're behind your mother one hundred percent," said Emily.

"Do you want to meet her?" asked Florence.

Emily's eyes lit up. "You bet."

"Come on."

Emily and Matt followed Florence out of the gallery and down the stairs to the first-floor chamber.

"Mama!" called Florence. She raced toward

her mother. Nellie was shaking hands with her supporters. She waved to her daughter.

The three children made their way through the crowd to reach Nellie. Florence threw her arms around her mother. "You were wonderful, Mama."

"I'm sure everyone wondered why I let Premier Roblin spout all that nonsense about women."

"I saw you watching him," said Florence.

Nellie laughed. "You're right. I watched every move he made. I listened to every untrue word and ridiculous comment."

Florence grinned. "Mama, these are my friends, Emily and Matt. They helped me deal with some nosy reporters in the gallery."

Nellie smiled. "Thank you for supporting Florence."

"We're behind you, Mrs. McClung," said

Matt. "Women deserve the same rights as men."

"That's what my family believes," said Emily.

Nellie beamed. "I wish more families believed in fairness for all. Then we wouldn't have to fight so hard."

"We heard about your play tomorrow, and we'd like to help," said Emily.

"Perhaps you can," said Nellie.

"Maybe they can stay over at our house tonight and help us plan," said Florence. "That is, if your family doesn't mind."

"They won't mind," said Matt.

"Check with them. If they'll let you join us, here's where we live," said Nellie. She wrote her address down on a scrap of paper.

"We'll be there soon," said Matt.

"Wonderful. It's important that the next generation stands up for equal rights. You are the future."

Arm in arm, Nellie and Florence walked out of the building.

"Now what?" said Matt. "We can't go over to the McClungs' right away. They think we're checking with our family."

"Let's walk around the block a few times and then head to their house," said Emily.

"Brrr…" said Matt, shivering. "It's too cold to walk outside."

"Then let's run around the block to stay warm. Race you!"

Matt picked up the sled. "One. Two. Three. Go!" he said.

Emily and Matt ran so fast they didn't see two tall boys chasing a smaller boy. The three boys zoomed toward them.

"Oh no!" cried Emily. They were about to collide with the small boy, but at the last second he managed to slip between Emily and Matt.

The two tall boys couldn't stop in time. They smashed right into Matt.

"Ouch!" cried Matt, clutching the sled. He tumbled into a mound of soft snow.

The two boys hit the ground hard.

"You…you…" sputtered one of the tall boys. His long brown bangs almost covered his eyes. He pointed a finger at Matt. "It's all your fault."

"My head. My head," moaned the other boy, who had thick blond hair. He took off his cap and rubbed his forehead.

"Sorry," said Matt. "We didn't see you." Matt stood up and brushed the snow off his clothes and the sled.

"We would have grabbed that stupid McClung kid if it hadn't been for you," snarled the boy with brown hair. "Where is he, anyway?" The boy looked around. There was no sign of the smaller boy.

"Come on, Jack," said the blond-haired boy. "We'll find him later. Let's go. My head feels like it's going to explode."

Jack stumbled to his feet. He glared at Matt. "We'll get you later. You'll be sorry you were in our way. Sal and I always come back, and we never forget."

The boys hobbled down the street.

"Are you okay?" Emily asked Matt, after they'd left.

Matt nodded. "I was lucky I fell in the

snowbank. And it's even luckier the sled is still in one piece. I was sure it would break when I fell. Those boys are mean. I wonder what happened to that boy they were chasing."

"They called him the McClung kid. Do you think he could be one of Nellie's children?" asked Emily.

"Yes!" said a voice. The smaller boy popped out from behind a large crate. He looked about ten. His pants were ripped at the knees.

"I'm Horace McClung," he said. "Jack and Sal waited for me after school. They called my mother names. I told them I was proud of my mother, and they threatened to punch me in the face. So I ran. If you hadn't been there…" Horace gulped. "They would have caught me for sure. Thanks."

5

No More Lies

"Wow!" said Emily. "You're Nellie McClung's son! We met your mother and sister today. We're going to your house to help with tomorrow's play."

Horace grinned. "That's terrific. I'll show you where we live."

The three children walked a few blocks. Soon they were in front of a three-storey clapboard house.

"Here's our home," said Horace. He opened the front door. "You can leave your sled here."

He pointed to a pile of boots, skates, and sleds in the front hall.

Emily and Matt placed the sled in a corner of the pile.

As they did, a red-haired man joined them. He stared at Horace and sighed. "Oh my. What happened to you? Don't tell me you've had another scuffle about your mother?"

"I did, Father. But I'm fine. My two new friends helped me."

Mr. McClung patted Horace on the back. "I'm glad you stood up for your mother, Son, but be careful. I don't want you to get hurt."

"But I can't let people tell lies about us. These two boys said that Mother neglected her family. Mother never neglects us."

"I know. Any time someone tries to change things, there are people who oppose it. Sometimes they even spread lies. I'm glad you found two friends to help you. So, Horace, introduce me."

"Emily and Matt, meet my father, Mr. Wes McClung."

"Nice to meet you, sir," said Matt, extending his hand.

Mr. McClung shook Matt and Emily's hands. "Thank you for helping my son."

"We're glad we were there," said Matt.

"And we were on our way here already, to help Mrs. McClung with the play," said Emily.

"Ah, the play!" said Mr. McClung, smiling. "Mrs. McClung is quite an actress. The audience is in for a big surprise. She's practising in the parlour right now. Let's go in and say hello."

The four headed down the hall to the parlour. Nellie was standing in front of a mirror with her thumb in the armhole of her jacket. She strutted around like she was an

important official. Then she wagged her finger in the air and puffed up her chest like Premier Roblin did this morning in the legislature.

"Excellent!" said Mr. McClung.

"Bravo!" said Horace.

Emily and Matt applauded.

"So do I remind you of the premier?" asked Nellie.

"Absolutely, except that you're much prettier, my dear," said her husband.

"Premier Roblin is going to hate it, Mother," said Horace.

"Good!" said Nellie. "He was so insulting today. Premier Roblin deserves to have fun poked at him. I hope the newspapers report everything we do tomorrow. Perhaps our premier will think twice before treating women like that again. Now, let's have dinner."

Everyone followed her into the dining room.

At dinner, they discussed how Emily and Matt could help Florence hand out pamphlets about women's rights at the theatre.

"But don't tell anyone that I'll be playing the premier," Nellie told them. "It's a surprise."

6

Worried

After dinner, Emily and Florence headed off to Florence's room. Emily waved good night to Matt. He was bunking with Horace and the other McClung boys.

Emily and Florence hopped up on Florence's bed. They talked about their plans for the play.

"Your mom is brave," said Emily.

"I know, but I'm worried about her. I keep telling myself that everything will work out, but there's still a knot in my stomach. Horace has been in three fights in just the last two weeks. Last month someone gave him a black eye! And people have made unkind remarks to Father. What if those reporters at the legislature are right? What if…"

Florence swallowed hard. Tears welled up in her eyes. Emily put her arm around her friend's shoulder.

"Your mom will be fine. Everything will work out. I know because…well, because…"

"Because what?" asked Florence, wiping her eyes with a handkerchief.

Emily took a deep breath. She slipped off the bed and walked over to her coat. She reached into the pocket and pulled out her sketchbook. She drew a quick picture of Matt standing in front of a car.

"Matt and I come from the future. See. That's a car from the twenty-first century. And I read about your mom in a book. She'll be famous for what she's doing to help women win rights."

Florence's eyes widened. She bit her lip as if she were trying not to laugh. "How did you get here from the...future?" she asked.

"We flew on our magic sled."

Florence burst into laughter. "Emily, you're wonderful."

"Wonderful?"

"You understand how worried I am about Mother, and you came up with this crazy story about the future. Imagine flying on a magic sled."

"I know it sounds crazy, Florence, but it's not a story. It happened. I didn't make it up."

"I appreciate what you're trying to do, but don't worry, Emily. I know it will be fine. Whatever happens, we all support Mother. What she's fighting for is important."

"But, Florence. It really is the truth. Matt and I *are* from the future."

Florence yawned. "Please, no more stories tonight, Emily. I'm tired. Let's go to sleep. Tomorrow will be a big day. And Emily..."

"What, Florence?"

"Thanks for making me laugh. I feel much better now. Good night."

Emily sighed. Maybe she should tell

Florence how she and her family flew to California on an airplane last year. Maybe she should try to describe television and computers. Emily peeked over at Florence. Her new friend was sound asleep.

Emily climbed into bed. She pulled the soft pink-and-white quilt over her shoulders and closed her eyes.

The next thing she knew, light was streaming through the window and someone was gently shaking her.

"Emily, wake up!" said Florence.

"What?" said Emily opening her eyes. "What happened?"

"Nothing happened," said Florence. "It's morning. Can you smell the coffee and bread? Our neighbour brought over a fresh-baked loaf of oatmeal bread. She came to wish us success tonight."

"See!" said Emily, slipping out of bed. "There are women all over Winnipeg who believe in your mother. Everything will be fine today."

"I hope so. I had a nightmare last night that someone threw a rock through our window and called Mother terrible names. I hope it was only a dream. I couldn't bear it if anything bad happened to anyone in our family—or to you and Matt."

7

Read All About It

The day flew by as everyone rushed to get ready for the play. Nellie practised her part. Emily, Matt, and Florence hand printed flyers about women's rights. They wrote, *Stand up for fairness. Support rights for all.*

At 5:30 they headed to the Walker Theatre.

"Look at the crowd here already!" said Matt, pointing to the people lining up for tickets.

"Every seat will be filled, Mother," said Florence.

"You're going to be bigger than a rock star!" said Emily.

Nellie laughed. "A rock star? Since when is a rock a star? What do you mean, Emily?"

Florence patted Emily on the back. "Emily's kidding, Mother. She loves making jokes. Yesterday she told me that she and Matt came here from the future. She said they flew to Winnipeg on a magic sled."

"I see," said Nellie. "So tell me, Emily, is being bigger than a rock star a good thing?"

Emily's face turned red. "It's very good. It means you'll have many fans, Mrs. McClung. Matt and I are your fans already."

"But I don't think Premier Roblin is ever going to be one of my fans," said Nellie.

"Who needs a fan like Premier Roblin anyway?" said Matt.

"You're right. We just need the legislature to change their attitude and laws, even if they're not happy about it," said Nellie. "I'm going to slip inside the back door of the theatre before anyone sees me. Promise me that you'll be careful."

The three children nodded. Nellie ducked into the theatre.

"Let's hand out our flyers and meet back here in twenty minutes," said Florence. "Then we can go into the theatre together."

Emily and Matt hurried to the front of the theatre and handed out the flyers. It was hard to move. The crowd rushed toward the entrance of the theatre.

"Stay close so we don't get separated," said Emily.

Matt nodded. "Read all about it!" he called. "Support women's rights!"

"Down with women's rights!" shouted two tall boys beside him.

Matt looked up. It was Jack and Sal! Matt looked around for Emily and Florence, but the crowd was so thick he couldn't see them, and he couldn't budge.

"We told you we'd be back," Jack barked. "And we always do what we say."

"Gimme those flyers," said Sal. He yanked a bunch of flyers out of Matt's hands. He ripped them into little pieces and tossed them in the air like confetti. "That's what we think of women's rights," he sneered.

Then he jabbed Matt in the shoulder.

8

Who Is She?

"Leave that boy alone, Sal!"

A short woman with long brown hair piled high on her head glared at Sal. She wagged her finger at him.

Sal's face turned red. "Miss Graham? I wasn't doing anything. I was just having a bit of fun."

"Poking people and ripping up their property is not fun. It's hooligan behaviour. You're not a hooligan are you, Sal?"

"No, ma'am. I just don't believe in this

women's rights business, and neither does my friend."

"What you or anyone believes does not give you the right to behave this way. I would hate to tell your parents about this. I suggest you leave and stop causing mischief."

"My pa doesn't believe in women's rights either."

"He may not, but your father would be furious if he heard that you were behaving like this. You don't want me to tell him, do you?"

"No, ma'am. We're leaving," he muttered.

But before they moved away, Jack whispered in Matt's ear. "We'll be back, and next time we'll do more than rip up your stupid papers." Then Jack and Sal pushed their way through the crowd.

Matt took a deep breath. "Thank you, Miss Graham," he said.

"I'm glad I could help. Sal is my student. I know he doesn't like school, but I never thought he'd behave this way. Look! The crowd is thinning. I hope I can get a ticket for the play."

"I hope so, too," said Matt. "I have to meet up with my friends. I'm sure you'll enjoy the show."

"I hope Nellie McClung will be in it," said Miss Graham. "I wish I could have heard her speak at the legislature, but I was teaching."

Miss Graham smiled. When she did, Matt knew he'd seen her somewhere before. But where? She hadn't gone to the legislature, and they hadn't gone anywhere else in Winnipeg except to the McClung's house.

"Thanks again, Miss Graham," Matt said. He wove his way back to the spot where the three friends were to meet.

Emily and Florence were waiting for him.

"What took you so long?" asked Emily.

"Those two bullies, Jack and Sal, showed up again. They ripped my flyers and poked me. But one of the boys' teachers stopped them. It was weird. She looked familiar."

"Maybe you met her in the future," said Florence, giggling.

"I don't think so," said Matt, "but I know I've seen her somewhere. She's a big fan of your mom's."

"That's wonderful," said Florence. "Let's hurry inside. The play is about to begin. Emily and I are going to be pages, the assistants in the legislature. Only girls can be pages in our play, Matt, but you can cheer us on."

Matt grinned. "I'll cheer so loud people will hear me all the way to the future."

"You two really love jokes," said Florence.

Emily winked at Matt. No one believed them about the future no matter what they said.

As they dashed into the theatre, Matt saw Miss Graham a few rows down. "There's the woman who helped me, Emily," he said. He waved to Miss Graham.

Miss Graham smiled and waved back.

"She does look familiar!" said Emily. "It's her eyes. They're so green. I've never seen anyone with such green eyes except people in your family, Matt."

"There was no one in my family named Graham," said Matt. "But I know I've seen her somewhere."

9

Finally

"Meet us at the back door after the play," said Emily.

Emily and Florence headed backstage to join Nellie. As Matt looked for a seat in the packed theatre, he glanced around for Jack and Sal. There was no sign of them anywhere.

Matt walked up and down the aisles, but there were no empty seats in the theatre. Finally, he found a spot to stand at the side. It wasn't far from the stage. He could see everything from there.

The lights dimmed. The audience hushed. The curtain rose and women in long black robes stood on stage. They were dressed like legislators.

The audience howled as the women actors portrayed stuffy politicians. And when Nellie walked on stage, the audience erupted in applause.

Nellie told the men on stage who asked her for votes that although they were good-looking fellows, that wasn't enough to give them the vote. She wagged her finger at them. She treated them like Premier Roblin had treated the women who'd asked him for rights.

Then she told the men they didn't need the vote anyway. After all, they had more important things to do, like support their families. It was silly of them to waste their time voting. Voting would wreck their homes and lives.

The audience loved every minute of the performance. They cheered as Nellie imitated the way the premier moved and talked.

Matt applauded till his hands hurt. He laughed till tears rolled down his cheeks.

"You think that's funny?" snarled someone behind him.

Oh no! Matt knew that voice. It was Jack. He and Sal stood so close to Matt, he could feel their breath on his neck.

"You liked that show? Well, how do you like this?" Sal stomped on Matt's toes.

"Cut that out," cried Matt.

"Why? Can't take a little pain?" sneered Jack. "What kind of boy are you?"

"Maybe you're not a boy after all," said Sal, pursing his lips and hissing into Matt's ear. "Maybe you're just a scared little girl."

10

Leave Me Alone

"Leave me alone," said Matt. He tried to squeeze away from the two bullies, but they blocked his way.

"We're not going anywhere," said Jack. "We're going to stop this stupid show."

Jack and Sal reached into their pockets.

What were they pulling out? What were they going to do?

And then Matt saw the eggs. They were going to toss them at the stage. They couldn't! They'd ruin everything.

"No!" said Matt. He whacked the eggs out of their hands. Sticky, raw egg splattered down Jack's pants and across Sal's jacket.

"Ugh!" screamed the two boys.

"Get off my foot!" screamed a woman behind them.

"Quiet," barked a man beside them.

In the commotion, Matt scooted away. He scurried out of the building and raced outside toward the back door of the theatre. He ran so fast that he stumbled and stubbed his toe, but he kept running.

All he could think about was that Jack and Sal might have left the theatre, too. They might be looking for him out here, and they were really angry with him now. Who knew what they might do next?

Matt reached the back door. He leaned against it to catch his breath. He tried to open the door, but it was locked. He peered around for Jack and Sal. No sign of them yet.

Applause rang out from inside the theatre. The play was still on but for how much longer? Matt banged on the door, but no one opened it.

Matt shivered. He clapped his hands together. They were starting to freeze. He jumped up and down to stay warm.

He banged on the door again. No one came.

He looked around for the two bullies. They might show up at any minute. And then what would he do? There was no one outside to help him.

The back door of the theatre creaked and then it opened.

"Emily!" said Matt.

"Wasn't the play wonderful?" she exclaimed, popping outside.

"It was great, but I didn't see the end of it." Matt quickly told her what had happened with Jack and Sal.

"Imagine if you hadn't stopped them from throwing eggs at the stage. They could have ruined everything. They must be really angry at you now."

"They are, and I bet they want to get me again. And I'm freezing. Let's go inside."

The friends hurried into the theatre.

"They won't be able to do anything to you here," said Emily. "There are lots of people around here who'll stop them."

"There's Florence and Mrs. McClung," said Matt. "And there's one of the reporters we spoke to at the legislature!"

It was Earl, the reporter with the moustache. He stopped Nellie as she dashed down the long hall toward the back door. "How does it feel to make fun of the Premier of Manitoba in public?" he asked her.

Nellie smiled. "All we really wanted to do was to make Mr. Roblin and all politicians recognize that women have rights, too."

"Do you think your performance will change the premier's mind?" asked the reporter.

"I have no idèa what will change the premier's mind, but with or without him women will continue to insist on being treated fairly. And we will continue to protest until we reach our goals."

"You were certainly a hit with the audience, Mrs. McClung. How do you feel about your wife's performance, Mr. McClung?"

"I am proud of Nellie," said Mr. McClung, smiling at his wife.

"And you kids, what do you think of Mrs. McClung?" the reporter asked Emily and Matt.

"We think she's awesome," said Matt.

"I know people will be talking about Nellie McClung and her play for a long time in the future," said Emily.

11

Crazy Story

Florence laughed. "There you go again, Emily. Talking about the future. Come on. Let's go home. Mother said we could have tea and carrot cake before we go to bed."

The three friends followed Mr. and Mrs. McClung down the street.

Florence pointed to a woman crossing the street. "There's Miss Graham. She's a teacher at my school."

"We met her in the theatre," said Matt. "She helped with some pushy boys."

"She's nice, but she won't be at school next year. She's marrying Mr. George Ross in the spring," said Florence.

Matt stared at Florence. "G...G...George Ross is marrying Miss Graham?" he stammered.

"Yes. Do you know him?"

"Sort of."

"How?"

"You're not going to believe me if I tell you."

"Is this another one of your crazy stories about the future?" asked Florence.

Matt nodded. "Yes, but it's true. George Ross was my great-grandfather, and Miss Graham must be my great-grandmother."

"I thought your family was from Mexico," said Emily.

"Half my family is from Mexico. The other half have lived in Canada for over a hundred years."

Florence rolled her eyes. "Enough crazy stories, you two! Let's have tea and cake. Mother makes wonderful creamy icing on her carrot cake. Wait till you taste it."

The children raced inside the McClungs' house. They took their boots off in the hall.

"Meet you in the kitchen," said Florence.

"Matt, look at the sled!" said Emily, when Florence left.

Shimmery gold words were forming on the front.

You stood for rights.
You let them know
That fair is fair.
It's time to go.

"We have to go home," said Emily. "Too bad! I wanted some of that cake."

"Me, too, but the sled wants us to go home. Let's write the McClungs a note."

Emily ripped a piece of paper out of her sketchbook. "Should we tell them the truth?"

Matt sighed. "Sure, but they won't believe us."

"Okay. Here's what I'm writing:

Dear McClung Family,

It was wonderful to meet you and terrific to be part of your fight for equal rights. We know you'll succeed. We wish we could stay longer, but we have to fly home.

Your friends,

Emily and Matt

Emily left the note on top of the pile of boots. Then she and Matt hopped on the sled. In an instant, it rose over the McClungs' house. As it flew over the street, Matt tapped Emily on the shoulder. "Look down there. It's Jack and Sal!"

Jack and Sal stood staring up at the sled. Their mouths hung open. They waved their fists at Matt and shouted something, but the sled was too high up for Emily or Matt to hear.

"They won't get you now," said Emily, laughing.

"They won't get me ever!" said Matt as the sled flew higher and into a fluffy white cloud.

12

The Picture

Soon the friends were back in Emily's tower. They hopped off the sled.

"That was a great adventure," said Emily. "Now I know exactly how Nellie McClung acted in the play. I'm going to practise her walk and talk in the mirror till I get it right."

"I was so busy trying to get away from Jack and Sal that I forgot to record anything, but I'll never forget what happened. Let's go to my house and ask my mom about Miss Graham. She would be on Mom's side of our family."

"Okay, but I'm starving. I was looking forward to Mrs. McClung's carrot cake with creamy icing."

"We can have apple cake at my house."

"Excellent!" said Emily. "I love apple cake."

The friends ran over to Matt's house.

"Look!" said Emily as they passed the front hall. She pointed to a picture on a low cabinet. "Isn't that...?"

Matt's eyes lit up. "It is! I forgot about that picture. There's Miss Graham beside my great-grandfather! She looks much older in the picture than when we met her. But this proves it! Miss Graham was my great-grandmother! I wish I could have told her about our family. I bet she'd think it was awesome that half of our family lived in Canada for years, and the other half came from Mexico twenty years ago."

"I bet she would, too," said Emily. "Now can we have cake?"

Matt grinned. "Do you want ice cream with your cake?"

"Mmmmm. Yes, please!"

"Chocolate or vanilla?"

"Hmmm..." said Emily, rubbing her chin. "It's a hard decision. But after careful consideration, I vote for one scoop of chocolate and one scoop of vanilla. How about you?"

"I second your vote," said Matt. "So now— let's eat!"

MORE ABOUT...

After their adventure, Matt and Emily wanted to know more about women's fight for rights. Turn the page for their favourite facts.

Emily's Top Ten Facts

1. Nellie Mooney was born in Ontario in 1873.

2. When she was seven, she and her family moved to Manitoba, where they hoped to find better land for farming.

3. Their first home in Manitoba was a log cabin with a thatched roof and only one window.

I hope it was a big window! —M.

4. Nellie first went to school near their family farm in Wawanesa, Manitoba when she was ten. She learned to read that same year, and loved reading her whole life!

5. She also loved the prairies, even though the summers could be hot and the winters were long and cold.

6. Nellie became a teacher at the age of sixteen and taught school 5 km (3 miles) from a small Manitoba town called Manitou.

7. In *1890* she met her future husband, Wes McClung, in Manitou. He had red hair and worked in a drugstore.

8. Nellie's first book, *Sowing Seeds in Danny*, was published in *1908* and became a bestseller.

9. Nellie and her family moved to Winnipeg in *1911*. In those days many of the people who moved to Winnipeg came from places such as Germany, Poland, Ukraine, Italy, and Russia.

10. Nellie once wrote: "Never retreat. Never explain. Never apologize. Get the thing done and let them howl."

Yay, Nellie!
—M.

Matt's Top Ten Facts

1. There were many more men than women living in Winnipeg when Nellie McClung moved there in 1911.

2. The word Winnipeg comes from the Cree language and means muddy waters.

3. Some people have nicknamed Winnipeg, Winterpeg. Guess why?

4. After World War I, a black bear named Winnipeg was donated to the London Zoo by Winnipeg Captain Harry Colebourn. That bear inspired English author A. A. Milne's famous stories about a bear called Winnie the Pooh.

I love Winnie The Pooh.
    -E.

5. Nellie McClung took Premier Roblin on a tour of factories to see the awful working conditions for women.

6. That trip to the factories made Nellie McClung realize that the premier had no interest in helping poor people, especially women.

How could he be so mean?
—E.

7. Premier Roblin once told this to Nellie McClung about women: "I don't want a hyena in petticoats talking politics at me...I want a nice, gentle creature to bring my slippers."

8. Nellie McClung said this about Canada: "I have seen my country emerge from obscurity into one of the truly great nations of the world."

9. Nellie McClung and her family moved to Alberta in 1916. She was elected to the Alberta legislature in 1921.

10. In June 2010, a monument was unveiled at the Manitoba legislature to honour Nellie McClung's contribution to Manitoba and Canada.

So You Want to Know...

FROM AUTHOR FRIEDA WISHINSKY

When I was writing this book, my friends wanted to know more about Nellie McClung and the women's rights movement. I told them that many of the characters in *Make It Fair!* were made up except for Nellie McClung, her family, and Premier Roblin of Manitoba.

Here are some other questions I answered:

Was Nellie McClung the first person to fight for women's rights in Canada?

No. Emily Stowe is considered the first. She was also the first woman in Canada to become a doctor. Emily Stowe founded the Toronto Literary Club in 1876, and in 1883 that club became the Canadian Women's Suffrage Association. Stowe's organization campaigned for women's rights and the right to vote.

Emily Stowe died in 1903 before she was able to achieve her goals and dreams, but the fight continued.

How did women "fight" for equal rights in Canada?

Canadian women and fair-minded men protested with petitions, lectures, and demonstrations until the law was changed. In Canada, the campaign for equal rights was peaceful, which wasn't always the case in other countries such as the United States and the United Kingdom.

When did women achieve the right to vote in Canada?

In 1916, the first Canadian province to give women the right to vote was Manitoba. It was an exciting day for women. All their work for equal rights finally paid off. And in 1918, women in Canada were given the right to vote in federal elections. But it still took a few years (and sometimes a lot more years) for the other Canadian provinces and territories to give women the vote in provincial elections. The Northwest Territories was last, finally granting women the right to vote in 1951.

Was that the end of the struggle for equal right and fairness for women?

No. Some laws and conditions for women in Canada remained unfair for many years. Although women could vote in most provinces, they couldn't run for government office. In 1927, Nellie McClung and four other women pushed the government in Ottawa to include women in the legal term "person" so they could run for office. This was called the "Persons Case." In 1929, because of the women's efforts, the law finally stated that women were "persons" just like men and could sit in the Senate.

Did women in other countries get the vote earlier than Canada?

In December 1869, Wyoming Territory (Wyoming hadn't yet become part of the United States) granted women the vote. But it wasn't until 1920 that all women in the U.S. were given the right to vote.

In 1893, New Zealand was the first country to give women the right to vote, but women couldn't run for office in New Zealand until 1919. In 1906, Finland was the first country to grant women the right to vote and to run for office. As for the United Kingdom, women were granted voting rights after World War I, in 1918.

What's the situation like today for women's rights?

Even today, women and men are not always treated equally. Sometimes women are not paid the same wage for the same work. Women in some countries today still have to fight for fair laws and equal rights.

Coming next in the
Canadian Flyer Adventures Series...

Canadian Flyer Adventures #16

Arctic Storm

Matt and Emily are in the Far North,
stranded in a ferocious blizzard.

For a sneak peek at the latest book in the series, visit:
www.owlkids.com
and click on the red maple leaf!

The *Canadian Flyer Adventures* Series

#1 Beware, Pirates!

#2 Danger, Dinosaurs!

#3 Crazy for Gold

#4 Yikes, Vikings!

#5 Flying High!

#6 Pioneer Kids

#7 Hurry, Freedom

#8 A Whale Tale

#9 All Aboard!

#10 Lost in the Snow

#11 Far from Home

#12 On the Case

#13 Stop that Stagecoach!

#14 SOS! Titanic!

#15 Make It Fair!

More Praise for the Series

"[Emily and Matt] learn more than they ever could have from a history textbook. Every book in this new series promises to shed light on a different chapter of Canadian history."
~ *Montreal Gazette*

"Readers are in for a great adventure."
~ *Edmonton's Child*

"This series makes Canadian history fun, exciting and accessible."
~ *Chronicle Herald (Halifax)*

"[An] enthralling series for junior-school readers."
~ *Hamilton Spectator*

"...highly entertaining, very educational but not too challenging. A terrific new series."
~ *Resource Links*

"This wonderful new Canadian historical adventure series combines magic and history to whisk young readers away on adventure...A fun way to learn about Canada's past."
~ *BC Parent*

"Highly recommended."
~ *CM: Canadian Review of Materials*

Teacher Resource Guides now available online. Please visit our website at **www.owlkids.com** and click on the red maple leaf to download tips and ideas for using the series in the classroom.

About the Author

Frieda Wishinsky, a former teacher, is an award-winning picture- and chapter-book author, who has written many beloved and bestselling books for children. Frieda enjoys using humour and history in her work, while exploring new ways to tell a story. Her books have earned much critical praise, including a nomination for a Governor General's Literary Award. She is the author of *Please, Louise; You're Mean, Lily Jean; Each One Special;* and *What's the Matter with Albert?* among others. Originally from New York, Frieda now lives in Toronto.

About the Illustrator

Patricia Ann Lewis-MacDougall started drawing as soon
as she could hold a pencil, and filled every blank spot in
her mother's cookbooks by the age of three. As she grew
up, Pat Ann never stopped drawing and enjoyed learning
all about the worlds of animation and illustration. She now
tells stories with her love of drawing and has illustrated
children's books and created storyboards for television
animation for shows such as *Little Bear* and *Franklin the
Turtle*. Pat Ann lives in Stoney Creek, Ontario.